W9-AXZ-644

STAR WARS™

MEET THE HEROES

CHEWBACCA

STAR WARS™

MEET THE HEROES

CHEWBACCA

Written by
Ruth Amos

What planet do Wookiees come from?

How old is Chewbacca?

Why should you let a Wookiee win a board game?

What's in Chewie's carry-pouch?

Can Chewie climb trees?

Find out the answers to these questions and many more inside!

Who is Chewbacca?

Chewbacca is a tall, furry, brave alien. He goes on many **adventures,** and helps his friends **save** the galaxy.

Does Chewbacca have a nickname?

Yes. His friends call him **Chewie.** It is quicker and easier to say than Chewbacca, especially during **dangerous missions** when there isn't much time for chatting!

7

What type of alien is Chewbacca?

He is a Wookiee. Wookiees are very tall, very strong, and extremely **hairy.** They may be **grumpy** at times, but they are brave and **loyal.**

Wookiees

What planet do Wookiees come from?

Kashyyyk. Chewie's homeworld is covered in forests of giant **trees.** This leafy planet has shallow **seas** and sandy **beaches.**

How tall is Chewbacca?

Extremely tall! Chewbacca's height is **2.3 meters** (7 feet, 7 inches) tall. He **towers** over most of the people that he meets.

Wicket

R2-D2

Luke Skywalker

Bossk

Chewbacca

11

How old is Chewbacca?

Chewie is 190 years old when he first meets his friend **Han Solo.** When the pair meets the Rebel Alliance group years later, Chewie is **200** years old.

So Chewbacca is really old?

Actually, no! Not for a Wookiee. Wookiees have **very long life spans.** This species usually lives for about **400** years.

Can Chewbacca climb trees?

Yes. Chewbacca has very strong, long **legs,** and his **toes** have **claws** that help him grip and climb. On Kashyyyk, Wookiees build their **homes** high up in the giant trees that grow there.

14

Why is Chewie so hairy?

Layers! Chewbacca's thick fur is made up of **three** layers. He has a **shaggy** outer coat, a middle layer, and a **soft** inner coat. All this fuzzy fur protects him from the cold and repels water.

Who calls him a "walking carpet"?

Princess Leia. She calls Chewie this after he rescues her from the Empire. This is the first time they meet. However, they soon become **good friends!**

Does he have a good sense of smell?

Yes. Chewie's nose is very **sensitive.** He can smell food from a long way away. Chewie's nose also helps him sniff out approaching **enemies.**

17

Why does Chewie make howling noises?

This is his language! It is called Shyriiwook (pronounced shree-wook). To human ears, it sounds like a series of **groans, growls,** and **howls.**

Does Chewie speak Basic?

No, he can't. Basic is the main language used by humans. Wookiees cannot speak Basic, due to the shape of their **vocal cords.** However, Chewie is still able to **understand** it!

19

What weapon is Chewbacca holding?

A bowcaster. This is a traditional Wookiee weapon, made by hand. It fires out **blast bolts** at great speeds. The bolts can **knock** armored soldiers off their feet!

Can anyone use a bowcaster?

They can try! However, a Wookiee's **great strength** is needed to wield one properly. Chewbacca's bowcaster is particularly **powerful,** and takes great skill to fire.

What does Chewie wear over his shoulder?

A bandolier. This long leather **strap** holds lots of silver-colored **cases.** Inside each case are the bolts that Chewie fires from his bowcaster.

What's in Chewie's carry-pouch?

Tools. Chewbacca is very good at **fixing** things. He likes to carry spare tools around with him, just in case he has to quickly **repair** his bowcaster or a ship.

Tools

Does Chewie have lots of friends?

Yes! During his adventures, he meets a gang of rebels. They work for the **Rebel Alliance.** Chewie joins his new friends on exciting missions to save the galaxy.

Leia   Luke

What is the Rebel Alliance?

A group of heroes. They try to protect the galaxy from the wicked Empire, and gain freedom for everyone. Many years later, Chewie and some of the rebels join the **Resistance.**

C-3PO   Poe   Rey   Finn

What is the Resistance?

Another group of heroes!

The Resistance battles the **First Order.**
This is an evil organization that seeks to
stamp out all of its enemies.

Where does Chewie first join the fight against the Empire?

On Kashyyyk. The Empire has a deadly **plot** to kill all the Jedi. The Jedi are Force-users who try to keep the peace. Chewie and the Wookiee chieftain, Tarfful, take the Jedi Master Yoda to a hidden **escape pod.** Yoda climbs inside it and **flies away** to safety.

Can a Wookiee fly a starship?

Definitely! Chewbacca is a **fantastic pilot.** He has spent many years flying starships. Chewie is the copilot of the *Millennium Falcon* and sits with the pilot in the cockpit.

What is the Millennium Falcon?

A very famous starship! The *Falcon* is one of the **fastest** ships in the entire galaxy. It is old and battered, but it has been upgraded many times with new technology. Han Solo **won** the ship from smuggler Lando Calrissian in a card game.

Who is Chewbacca's best friend?

Han Solo, of course! Han is a **smuggler** and a **pilot.** He is a human, and he comes from the planet Corellia. Chewie and Han go on lots of adventures together.

Where do they meet?

In a prison cell! Poor Chewbacca is being held captive in a **wet, muddy pit** by the evil Empire on the planet Mimban. The Imperial officers call Chewie **"the Beast."**

How does Han end up in the pit?

Bad behavior! Han works as a soldier for the Empire. He gets into **trouble** with an officer, and is **dumped** into the muddy prison cell with Chewie.

How do they escape?

Teamwork. Han convinces Chewie that they must **trust** each other and work together. Chewie **pushes over** a big pillar that holds up the roof of the cell. The roof collapses and they climb out.

What is Han and Chewie's first job together?

Chewie and Han join a gang of outlaws. They plan to steal some valuable **fuel** from a fast-moving Imperial vehicle on the snowy planet of Vandor.

Is it dangerous?

It's very risky! Chewbacca and Han must find the wagon that holds the fuel. They have to fight off the Empire's **range troopers,** and try not to **fall off** the speeding vehicle!

Does Chewie get his hands on the fuel?

Almost! Super-strong Chewie detaches the wagon from the rest of the train. Then **disaster** strikes! The wagon falls and all the fuel is lost in an **explosion.**

33

Who are Han and Chewbacca speaking to here?

A Jedi named Obi-Wan Kenobi

and his friend, Luke Skywalker. They are in the Mos Eisley Cantina bar on the planet Tatooine. This bar is a good place to make **deals.** They ask Han and Chewbacca for a **ride** in the *Millennium Falcon*.

Why should you let a Wookiee win a board game?

Wookiees are bad losers.

They really **hate** losing games. If you ever play a game of **holochess** with Chewbacca, it is best to let him win!

How often does Chewbacca rescue his friends?

Many times! One time, Chewie and Han protect Luke's **starfighter** vehicle from Darth Vader's TIE fighter during the Battle of Yavin. Luke is able to blow up the Empire's **Death Star** battle station.

Has Chewie ever saved a princess?

Of course! When Princess Leia is a prisoner on the Death Star, Chewbacca goes on a **mission** with Luke and Han to rescue her. They all escape together!

How does Chewie end up in a trash compactor?

It's a long story! Chewie and the rebels try to escape from the Death Star. They jump down the **garbage chute** and land in the trash compactor. It's very **smelly** inside!

40

Can Chewbacca fix a starship?

Yes! Chewie is an excellent **mechanic.** He makes repairs to the *Millennium Falcon* and keeps it running smoothly.

41

Who says "Laugh it up, fuzzball!" to Chewbacca?

It's Han! He tries to show off in front of Princess Leia, but she is not impressed and calls Han a **"laser brain."** Chewbacca thinks this is really **funny.** Han is not happy with his friend!

Can he fix a droid?

Sort of! When C-3PO is broken into pieces, Chewie tries to put the parts back together. However, he screws C-3PO's head on **backward!**

Why is Chewie carrying C-3PO like a backpack?

He runs out of time to fix him! The rebels are in danger and must **escape** quickly. Chewie decides to carry C-3PO on his back and finish fixing him later!

43

Which battles does Chewbacca fight in?

Many. The Wookiees defend their homeworld from a **droid army** during the Battle of Kashyyyk. Chewie also fights **stormtroopers** during the Battle of Takodana. These are only two!

Do Chewie and his friends always win battles?

Sadly, no! Chewbacca helps defend the rebels' base from the Empire's vehicles and soldiers on the **snowy** planet Hoth. However, the Imperial attack is too strong. The rebels are **forced** to run away.

What makes Chewbacca lose his temper?

Other people! Chewbacca is usually calm and peaceful, but he can get very grumpy if people are **unkind** to him or **annoy** him.

Why does Chewie get mad at Lando?

He betrays the rebels. Lando is supposed to be Han's **friend,** but he hands over the rebels to evil Darth Vader. Vader takes them all **prisoner!** Chewbacca is very angry with Lando.

Is Chewie brave?

Extremely! Chewbacca is not afraid to put himself in danger for others. He **volunteers** to join a rebel strike team. The team goes on a **dangerous** mission to the moon of Endor.

Why is the mission dangerous?

It's super risky! The team must fly a stolen shuttle to Endor. Then they must **sneak** up to an Imperial base and take control of it. The fate of the galaxy **depends** on them!

Is Chewie loyal?

Definitely. Chewie helps his friends and allies through **trouble** and tricky moments, over and over again. Chewbacca **loves** his friends and would never desert them.

Why does Chewbacca pretend to be a prisoner?

To get into Jabba's palace. Jabba the Hutt is a gangster who has captured Han. Leia **disguises** herself as a bounty hunter and **pretends** she has caught Chewie. Leia sells Chewie to Jabba as part of their plan to free Han.

Why is it not a good idea to put Chewbacca in handcuffs?

It makes him angry. Handcuffs **remind** poor Chewbacca of the time that he spent as a **slave** of the Empire.

51

What does Chewie like to eat?

Many tasty things.

Wookiees eat plants, meat, and berries. They love **spicy, hot food**. Chewie cooks a cute **porg** bird on the planet Ahch-To. He feels a bit guilty!

Does his hunger ever lead to trouble?

Sadly, yes. Hungry Chewie finds some meat in the forest on Endor. Unfortunately it is a **trap** set by Ewoks. When Chewie touches the food, the rebels are caught in a **big net!**

How does Chewie surprise the Empire?

By stealing one of their vehicles!

Chewbacca **takes over** an AT-ST (All Terrain Scout Transport) walker. He fires its **cannons** at the Empire's other walkers and soldiers, and knocks them down.

Who does Chewie fly ships with?

It depends. Chewie usually flies the *Falcon* as the copilot of **Han Solo.** But later, Chewie shares the cockpit with **Rey.** She is a very talented pilot.

Is Chewbacca a good patient?

Not really! He doesn't often get injured, so when he does, he **moans** about it!

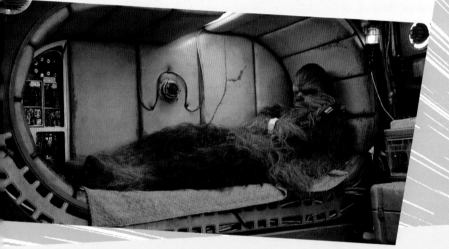

How does Finn try to help him?

With a bandage! Chewie's arm is wounded in a fight with a gang of **criminals.** Finn tries to put a bandage on it, but Chewie is scared and grumpy. He keeps **attacking** poor Finn.

So how do you help a wounded Wookiee?

With kindness! Doctor Kalonia treats Chewie's injuries after the Battle of Takodana. She **listens** to Chewie's howls and calms him down. She tells him that he has been very **brave.**

How does Chewie help destroy Starkiller Base?

With a smart plan. Han and Chewie secretly place **explosives** around the First Order's base. Chewie presses a detonator. The explosion makes a big **hole.** Then the Resistance's pilots can attack the base from space.

Does Chewie ever run from danger?

Not without his friends! When Starkiller Base **crumbles** apart, Rey and wounded Finn have no way to escape. Chewie arrives in the *Millennium Falcon* to save them, **just in time.**

What's next for Chewbacca?

A big escape! The First Order is attacking the Resistance on the planet Crait. Chewie pilots the *Falcon* and **leads** the enemy's ships away from the battle. The surviving rebels board the *Falcon* and Chewie flies away. His friends are safe... **for now!**

Glossary

Betray
To not be loyal to a friend or an organization that you are part of.

Bounty hunter
Someone who tracks down, captures, or kills people in exchange for money.

Empire
A group of nations ruled over by one leader, who is called an Emperor.

Fuzzy
Covered in fine hair or fur.

Holochess
A board game in which holographic creatures fight each other.

Imperial
Belonging to the Empire.

Range trooper
A special type of stormtrooper who wears heavy armor and fur.

Repel
To keep something out, or be resistant to something.

Smuggler
Someone who moves goods illegally between places and sells them for a profit.

Stormtrooper
A soldier used by the Empire.

Vocal cords
Parts of the voice box, located inside the throat. They vibrate to create sound and help produce the voice.

Senior Editors Ruth Amos and Emma Grange
Senior Designers Lynne Moulding and Clive Savage
Project Art Editor Jon Hall
Designers David McDonald and Stefan Georgiou
Senior Pre-Production Producer Jennifer Murray
Senior Producer Jonathan Wakeham
Managing Editor Sadie Smith
Managing Art Editor Vicky Short
Publisher Julie Ferris
Art Director Lisa Lanzarini
Publishing Director Simon Beecroft

DK would like to thank: Sammy Holland, Michael Siglain, Troy Alders, Leland Chee,
Pablo Hidalgo, and Nicole LaCoursiere at Lucasfilm; Chelsea Alon at Disney Publishing;
and Lori Hand and Jennette ElNaggar for editorial assistance.

First American Edition, 2019
Published in the United States by DK Publishing
1450 Broadway, Suite 801, New York, NY 10018

ISBN: 978-1-4654-8569-4

DK books are available at special discounts when purchased in bulk for sales promotions,
premiums, fund-raising, or educational use. For details, contact: DK Publishing Special
Markets, 1450 Broadway, Suite 801, New York, NY 10018, SpecialSales@dk.com

Printed and bound in China